THE RUNAWAY
CANDY CANE

A Christmas Tale by

Jeff White

ISBN-13: 978-0-9960337-1-8

10 9 8 7 6 5 4 3 2 1   11 12 13 14 15 16
Printed in the U.S.A.
First softcover edition, November 2016

for
Luke, Daisy & Cooper

THE RUNAWAY
CANDY CANE

Chapter One

THE
KITCHEN

The journey from the candy factory to the delivery truck to the supermarket to the station wagon to the kitchen counter was all a blur. Jay the candy cane didn't remember much about that part of his story. But he'll never forget the rest of it.

Jay blinked when the lights flickered on. The kitchen was a bright, cheery place, full of colors and shapes he'd never seen before. The other nine candy canes in his box were amazed.

"Wow," said one.

"This is one heck of a paradise!" said the second.

"This place is too glorious for … for … for …." stuttered the third.

"Words," added the fourth.

"We're in heaven!" said the fifth.

"I think we'll be quite happy here," beamed the sixth candy cane.

"No doubt about it," nodded the seventh.

"Vrrrumphfermmumbber," garbled the eighth, who hadn't yet learned to talk.

"Is that a jar of pickles?" the ninth one said.

Jay didn't know what to say. He smiled on the inside as he soaked it all in. This was so much more wonderful than the supermarket shelf he'd been sitting on the last two months. His view across the aisle had been of little more than jumbo packs of diapers and Ultra-Sensitive Double-Organic Free-Range Kale-Seed-Oil Baby Wipes, and he didn't like to imagine what those might be used for.

But this! This house was bursting with Christmas. The frills and trimmings were everywhere: garland, tinsel, stockings, wreaths, bows, lights, mistletoe, candles, poinsettias, gingerbread, ornaments, bells, holly, mittens, snowflakes, ribbons, stars, cranberries, chestnuts, tin soldiers, nutcrackers, angels, elves, reindeer, twinkles, jingles, and more red noses than should be allowed.

The best part of all was the Christmas Tree. He could barely see it through the kitchen door, twinkling and shining like a crown of a thousand jewels. That was where he wanted to be. Soon he would be hanging on that tree, putting a smile on every face and bringing families together in a halo of endless joy. It was what he was made for.

Until the most upsetting, disgusting, horrible thing happened.

The lady who brought them home put a big bowl on the counter and began to pour ingredients into it — eggs, vanilla, and lots of white powders.

"I wonder what she's making?" said the first candy cane.

"Heck if I know," said the second.

"She must be making some kind of … of … of …." stuttered the third.

"Christmas cookies," said the fourth.

"Mmm! I wonder if we can eat them?" asked the fifth.

"I'll bet they're delicious!" beamed the

sixth.

"No doubt about it," nodded the seventh.

"Grrmmblerblummffyvermmermm," the eighth mumbled.

"I wish I could eat those pickles," said the ninth.

Jay stared at the lady as she stirred and mixed the cookie dough. He didn't know why, but he had an uneasy feeling about it.

Chapter Two

THE
HORROR

The lady opened the box of candy canes and pulled one out.

"Woohoo! I get the first taste!" candy cane number one said. But he was very, very wrong.

The lady put him in a plastic bag and zipped it closed. Then she lay it on the counter and began whacking the candy cane into tiny bits with a large spoon.

"WHAT IN THE HECK —" shrieked the second candy cane.

"SOMEONE COVER MY … MY … MY …." stuttered the third.

"EYES!" shouted the fourth.

"THIS CAN'T BE HAPPENING!" wept the fifth.

"WE'RE ALL GONNA DIE!" screamed the sixth.

"NO DOUBT ABOUT IT," nodded the seventh.

"DRRBBLLLWWRRRBBBLLLFFF!" muttered the eighth.

"ARE THE PICKLES OKAY?" yelled the ninth.

Jay couldn't believe what he was seeing. In mere seconds, the first candy cane had become a small pile of peppermint dust. The lady (or, as the candy canes now called her, the Evil Mistress of Christmas Horrors) unzipped the bag and poured the dead candy cane's crushed remains into her bowl of cookie dough. Then she whistled a cheerful holiday tune as she stirred them in.

She actually whistled!

"I gotta get out of here," Jay said.

He glanced to the left and to the right, looking for the fastest way to make his escape. Just then, the Evil Mistress of Christmas Horrors stopped stirring, put down her Wicked Spoon of Death, and yanked candy cane number two out of the box.

"Aw, heck," the candy cane said right before she tossed him into her plastic bag and smashed him into a thousand pieces.

"Nuts to this," Jay said, and while the lady was sprinkling candy cane number two into her dough, he took a deep breath and jumped out of the box.

"Where are you going, you … you … you …." stuttered the third candy cane.

"Coward," said the fourth.

"You're not supposed to do that!" the fifth one said.

"You'll just make things worse," cried the sixth.

"No doubt about it," said the seventh.

"Ufffkkknnnburfffmmllll!" garbled the eighth.

"Can you get me a pickle?" asked the ninth.

Jay glanced back at his candy canes buddies and said, "No way I'm getting smashed into sprinkles. I'm heading for that Christmas Tree. See you fellas later!"

Or not, he thought.

Chapter Three

THE
GINGERBREAD MAN

Jay ducked behind the candy cane box. He could hear the other candy canes whispering to each other, but couldn't understand what they were saying. If they were smart, he thought, they would run away with him. But he wasn't going to wait around to find out.

He darted around the cookie jar and then side-stepped his way past the wooden knife block, shocked at the number of knives the

Evil Mistress of Christmas Horrors kept in her kitchen. Quick as he could, Jay slipped behind the spice rack and crawled along the wall to the end of the counter. Then he peered over the edge.

It was a long, long way down. If Jay jumped, he would surely shatter into at least 187 pieces. He preferred to remain in one piece, thank you very much. There must be another way down, Jay thought. But how?

He looked all around, up and down the counter. Through the kitchen door he could see the twinkling lights of the Christmas Tree. That was his goal. Then he spotted it: a jumbo bag of marshmallows. If he could push them over the edge, he could jump and land on them like a fluffy pillow.

Jay peeked at the Evil Mistress of Christmas

Horrors. She had just shoved candy cane number three into her Vile Baggie of Doom, and was now whacking him mercilessly with her Wicked Spoon of Death. How much peppermint did those cookies need, anyway? No time to lose, he said to himself.

He crawled across the counter in the direction of the marshmallows, slinking his way around three cans of cranberry sauce and squeezing between two boxes of crackers. When he reached the bag of marshmallows, he leaned up against it and pushed with all his strength. It barely budged.

"Drat!" Jay said. "Now what am I going to do?"

"Hey!" came a gruff voice behind him. "What'choo doin' there, buddy?"

Jay spun around to come face to face with

a gingerbread man. And it wasn't a cute little smiley gingerbread man like he'd seen on the back of the bag of flour. It was a lumpy, misshapen, and burnt gingerbread man with droopy licorice eyes and a crooked frosting mouth. Jay was a little afraid of him.

"I'm, um, trying to move this bag of marshmallows," Jay said less than bravely. "And, as a matter of fact, I could use your help."

"Choo ain't doin' nothin' with those mushmillers," said the gingerbread man, pointing his bulging hand in Jay's face. "Choo gonna get back in yer box where ya belong, buddy."

"Nope. No way. Never gonna happen," Jay said, shaking his head. "I'm NOT going to be murdered for some dumb dessert."

"Look, buddy, don't make it harder on yourself than it has to be. Just do what yer supposed to do and everyone's happy."

"That's easy for you to say. You're not being made into cookies!" Jay said.

"I AM a cookie. Now get movin'," said the gingerbread man.

He reached to grab Jay, but Jay jumped out of reach.

"Now wait just a minute!" Jay said, his back against the bag of marshmallows. "You gotta understand. I'm a candy cane! I belong on the Christmas Tree!"

"Everything has its place, buddy, and your place is in your box." The gingerbread man lunged at and missed Jay again, but this time he landed hard against the marshmallows, pushing them partway off the counter. Jay saw his chance. He circled around the gingerbread man till he was in front of the bag again. His face looked really angry now, and Jay knew he'd have to be fast.

"When I catch'oo, I'm gonna turn you into bits and pieces myself!" growled the gingerbread man, and then he rushed at Jay a third time. But this time, he caught Jay with one hand, and then Jay, the gingerbread man, and the bag of marshmallows all fell to the floor together.

The marshmallows were fine, of course. Jay landed right on top of them, bounced once, and made it safely to the ground. The gingerbread man, however, was not so lucky. He landed just past the bag of marshmallows, hitting the floor and breaking into seven pieces.

"You're spoiling everything," groaned the gingerbread man's face, which had broken off its body. "Just go back to where you belong."

"I'm sorry," Jay said. "I didn't mean for this to happen. Maybe the lady can glue you back together with some frosting?"

The gingerbread man mumbled something more, but Jay didn't stick around to listen. He ran as fast as he could to the kitchen table, where he tried to catch his breath. As he peered out through the forest of chair legs, he could just make out the bottom of the Christmas Tree and the lowest string of blinking lights. It looked far away, but nothing was going to keep Jay from getting there and making it his home.

THE
NUTCRACKER

Jay glanced back toward the kitchen and saw the red velvet shoes of the Evil Mistress of Christmas Horrors. She was still busy with her Mixing Bowl of Mayhem, and he couldn't help wondering how many of his other candy cane friends had been murdered. But he wasn't going to let that happen to him. He wanted to shine and glow with holiday cheer!

He wanted to get on that dang-blasted Tree, doggonit!

To get there, Jay had to stay out of sight. He scanned the area in front of him, looking for shadows or objects he could hide behind as he made his way to the Tree. He didn't see much — a hat rack, a potted plant, a big nutcracker, and a bit farther out, a china cabinet. There were plenty of dark shadows under the cabinet, but Jay would be exposed until he reached it. The nutcracker stood halfway to the cabinet. Perhaps it could keep Jay safe for a quick moment before he sprinted to the shelter of the cabinet.

Jay took a deep breath, glanced from side to side, then took off for the nutcracker. The polished wood floor was slippery, but Jay managed to reach the tall, rigid soldier in just a few seconds. The nutcracker was nearly two feet tall, painted in glossy green, red, and blue, with furry black boots, a tall black hat with an emerald feather, and a bushy white eyebrow. He stared straight ahead, as if he were a guard on watch.

After taking a moment to catch his breath, Jay looked up at the nutcracker and said, "Hi there!"

The nutcracker looked down, cleared his throat, and said nothing. He returned to staring forward, seemingly at nothing in particular.

"You're a Christmas decoration, right?" asked Jay.

"I most certainly am NOT," huffed the nutcracker.

"You look rather Christmassy."

"I, sir, am a nutcracker."

"What do you do?"

"I crack nuts."

"Are you sure? Because I just saw the lady in the kitchen cracking lots of nuts without you."

"I don't believe it."

"I've seen them. The cracked nuts."

"Impossible."

"Pecans, hazelnuts, almonds. Even walnuts. All got cracked."

"I'm sure she's saving me for the special nuts."

"You mean the big ones? Like Brazil nuts?"

"The bigger the better."

"Brazil nuts are gross. No one eats those."

"Regardless, I'll be ready to crack them when the time comes."

"Have you actually ever cracked a nut before?"

The nutcracker frowned. "Like I said, she's saving me for something special."

"Right. Down here on the floor next to the house plant. That's reeaalllly special."

"And what, may I ask, makes you so special?" asked the nutcracker.

"All the other candy canes got smashed up and put into cookies. But not me! I'm on my way to the Christmas Tree. I'm going to hang there and be a beautiful decoration and bring shiny joy to the world," Jay said, beaming.

"It looks to me like you're a runaway. A fugitive. A deserter," the nutcracker said, looking down on Jay with his bushy brow furrowed.

"I'm not a deserter! I don't want to be in any desserts!"

"That's not what I—"

"Anyway, I was wondering if you could point me to the safest way to get to that big room with the Christmas Tree. I need to get there unseen. And also fast. But mostly unseen."

"I most certainly will NOT help you. Every Christmas treasure has its special place. Your place is in those cookies. You should march right back in that kitchen and—"

"Well anyhoo, I gotta run. While you're waiting around not cracking any nuts, I'll be basking in all my yuletide glory right in the smack center of that Tree."

"But—"

"May you and the houseplant have a nut-free Merry Christmas together!" said Jay with a wave.

Chapter Five

THE
COAL CAR

Jay headed straight for the china cabinet. In two shakes of a reindeer's tale, he was standing in the safety of its shadows. He looked behind him to make sure he wasn't followed. When he turned back around, he came face to face with a toy train car. Jay jumped in surprise.

"Who are you?" Jay asked, still shaking from the shock.

"I'm the coal car," she said.

"The coal car?"

"From the Christmas train."

"Why are you under here?"

"I got kicked under here accidentally by one of the kids. It was an accident. A freaking freak accident."

"So why aren't you with the rest of the train?"

"This is my place now. Everything has its place."

"Your place is hidden and forgotten under the cabinet?"

The coal car frowned while she stared at the ground. "It's . . . safe."

"Isn't it lonely?"

"A bit."

"You're awfully dusty. How long have you been under here?"

"About three Christmases, I think."

"Three Christmases?! That's a long time!"

"But now you're here. You'll be my friend, won't you?" asked the coal car.

Jay peeked out beyond her toward the living room. He could just barely see one low branch of the Tree, and a single red light blinking off and on. He felt his heart beating in sync with the twinkling bulb. He was getting closer, but still had a ways to go.

"Look, you seem like a nice train toy and everything. The nicest I've ever met, to tell the truth. But—"

"You're not leaving me, are you?" said the coal car. Her lip quivered and her eyes welled up with coal-colored tears. "You're the first friend I've seen in three years. Except for that lost nickel over there, but he doesn't talk much."

"I'd love to stay, but my place is on that Tree. It's my heart's deepest desire. My dream. My destiny."

"Oh, I wish I could go with you!"

"You have wheels, you know. Just roll on over there."

"I can't move without my engine. I'm just a coal car."

"Hm. I'll tell you what. If I see the engine, I'll let him know you're here."

"HER. The engine's a she," said the coal car.

"Her. Right. I'll tell HER you're here, and she and the rest of the train will come get you."

"But there aren't any tracks over here. The engine can't run without tracks."

"I'm running without tracks. I'm not even

supposed to have legs."

"So you're breaking up with me?" A black tear dropped from the coal car's eye.

"Whoa, whoa, little lady choo-choo. I just met you, like, ten seconds ago. There's no breaking up, no breaking down, no breaking sideways. . . ."

"Never mind. I'll be fine. All by myself. Alone. Forsaken and friendless."

"Gosh, I'd help you if I could, really. But I gotta get going. Maybe I'll see you around sometime?"

And then Jay rushed to the far side of the cabinet without so much as a glance backward.

Chapter Six

THE
CAT

Jay inched toward the edge of the shadows, keeping himself hidden on the back side of the cabinet. He'd made it this far, and was determined not to get caught. The tree was still within sight. And now he thought he could hear the faint sound of Christmas music drifting from the living room.

He could see the door to the living room, but it was only slightly closer. He searched for another safe stretch of ground to cover. Next to the cabinet stood a sliding glass door — no hiding place there, but there was a curtain on the other side of it. In front of the curtain sat a small bowl of water and a little food bowl with the name "Princess Poopsie-Fangs" written on the side.

"Hm," thought Jay. "There must be a cat or a dog or a koala around here somewhere. I better be careful. But," he chuckled, "I guess I don't need to be afraid of anyone named Princess Poopsie-Fangs."

Jay was wrong.

He looked both ways to make sure no one was in the area. Then he sprinted across the long stretch of the sliding glass door toward the curtain. Just as he was about to reach the edge of the curtain, he was stopped by an enormous hairy face baring a wide set of crooked, sharp teeth. Even though the black-and-gray cat was wearing a red velvet bow with a jingle bell around its neck, the hair on its back stood on end, and its tail swished back and forth like a whip.

"P-Princess P-Poopsie F-Fangs!" Jay stuttered. He froze where he stood, unsure of what cats do to candy canes. At the moment it didn't seem to like them much. Its left eye was twitching as it slowly raised its paw. Jay got the feeling it was going to take a swipe at him.

"Niiiiice kitty," said Jay.

The cat swung at him anyway. But Jay was faster, and leaped out of its reach just in time. In two steps and a jump, he landed in the cat's water bowl, splashing it in the face. Princess Poopsie-Fangs sprung backward, shaking the water off its whiskers. The extra milliseconds were just enough time for Jay to hop out of the bowl and dive behind the curtain. He stood as still as an icicle at the North Pole, although his heart was beating as if it were on fire. He heard the cat let out a growling meow. He waited until he heard the cat's bell jingle fade into the distance.

Jay let out a long breath and shook his head. Following his dreams was turning out to be dangerous work. He was going to have to be even more careful. But even a twitchy-eyed cat wasn't going to keep him from getting to that Tree.

Chapter Seven

THE
CHOCOLATES

He stayed close to the wall as he made his way behind the curtain. When he reached the end, he peeked out. Jay was relieved to find a short bench along the wall. Beyond the bench, past a cluster of shopping bags and down a short hallway, awaited the entryway to the glorious epicenter of his holiday universe. The Tree itself was no longer in view, but the Christmas music was the tiniest bit louder —

something cheerful with drums and bells. The Tree was closer … but still so far away.

He could also see a gray-and-black-striped tail on the other side of the room. The cat's body was hidden behind a basket of hats and mittens, but Jay knew he needed to keep up his guard. He also needed to stay out of sight. Walking under the bench left him in plain site. He'd have to climb up on the bench and make his way across it like a bridge. Hopefully he'd find another safe place to sneak through.

It took some tricky jumping and waggling, but soon Jay found himself atop the bench. It was lined with holiday pillows of every color, and in the center of the bench sat a cardboard Advent calendar. He was tempted to sneak behind the pillows, but he wanted to see the calendar up close. The art on the box was a fancy painting of an adorable Christmas village, filled with Victorian houses covered in wreaths and strings of lights, pine trees dotted with red and white bows, sleighs pulled by horses, and a busy ice rink right in the middle. Several of the paper flaps were open, and all were empty except for one, which contained a moon-shaped chocolate.

"HI!" said the little chocolate. Jay jumped in surprise. "Who are you?!?" it asked, far more loudly than necessary.

"Shh! Keep it down!" Jay whispered back. "You'll wake the cat!"

"Princess Poopy-Butt?" said the chocolate. "She doesn't even like chocolate."

"She doesn't like me, either," said Jay. "At least, she didn't say she did."

"Cats don't talk, silly," said the chocolate

moon.

"But we do!" said several voices from inside the box.

"Who are you talking to?" called one squeaky voice.

"Did you meet another chocolate?" said another.

"Will someone please open my flap?" shouted a third voice. "I'm a week late!"

"Are those friends of yours?" Jay asked.

The chocolate moon rolled his eyes. "Friends. Neighbors. Cousins. Something like that. Anyway, who are you?"

"I'm Jay. I'm a candy cane."

"I can see that. Peppermint, right?"

"Yes. Aren't they all?" Jay asked.

"They've got fruit-flavored ones nowadays!" said one of the chocolates inside the box.

"Like orange!" said a second.

"Or watermelon!" said a third.

"And green tea acai with chia seeds!" said a fourth. "No, really, it's a thing."

"So what are you doing on our bench, Mr. Peppermint?" said the chocolate moon.

Jay pointed to the door down the hall. "I'm making my way to the Christmas Tree. I'm gonna be a decoration!"

"A decoration? But you're candy. Isn't candy supposed to get eaten?" asked the chocolate moon.

"Not me! I'm going to hang on that tree and be an inspiration to millions of people!"

All the chocolates inside the box laughed.

"What's so funny?" asked Jay.

"Candy is for eating. That's what we're for, you and us. Everything has its place. And that's our place," the chocolate moon said.

"Do you even know what it means to be eaten?" Jay asked.

"Joy!" said a chocolate inside the box.

"Delight!" said another.

"Happiness!"

"Heaven!"

Jay shook his head. "Maybe for the eater. But not for you."

The chocolate moon frowned. "What do you mean?"

"I'll tell you what happens. They take you and put you in their mouth, where you start to melt. But before you can melt all the way they chew you up into a thousand gooey bits with their razor-sharp teeth. And then they swallow you into their dark, churning guts, where you transform into—and I'm not even kidding—stinky, slimy turdlings!"

All the chocolates were silent for a long moment. Finally the chocolate moon spoke up.

"That's not what they told us at the chocolate factory," he said. "They said eating was fun."

"I'm sorry to sound so grim, but that's how it is. If everything has its place, then your place is … not pleasant. I can't polish it to make it sound any better."

"I don't want to be a turdling," said a hushed voice from inside the calendar.

"Me neither! That's why I'm heading for the Tree. It's safe there," said Jay.

The chocolate moon looked glum. "Well, everything has its place. And this is our place, fellas. The people seem to have forgotten about us anyway. They're not even opening our flaps anymore. So maybe won't get eaten after all."

"We'll just get thrown in the trash after Christmas is over," said a gloomy voice inside.

Jay wrung his hands and began to sidle toward the other end of the bench. "Well, anyway, the big day is tomorrow, so I better keep going. See you chocolates later. Merry … Christmas … or whatever."

As Jay rounded the Christmas pillows along the bench, he couldn't help feeling sad. The chocolates were so merry when he met them, but now they were miserable. Although he didn't mean to, he had spoiled their Christmas. He had stolen their joy. He wondered if there might be a way to make it up to them, but nothing came to mind. Jay sighed. For now, he needed to press on toward his goal.

No matter what.

Chapter Eight

THE
SLIPPERS

When he reached the last pillow, he looked back to where the cat had been hiding. Princess Poopsie-Fangs' tail was no longer in sight. Jay wasn't sure if that was good or bad. Maybe the cat had gone. Or maybe it was waiting nearby to ambush him.

He swallowed hard and peeked over the edge of the bench. Although he couldn't see any sign of the cat, he wasn't sure whether the cat was waiting below. He listened for sounds of purring or a tail swishing, but the only noise he heard was the gentle singing of a Christmas carol from the radio in the living room.

Jay held his breath, gripped the side of the bench, and slid down. As soon as he hit the floor, he spun around in all directions, looking for the cat. Thankfully, there was no sign of Princess Poopsie-Fangs.

Not too far away was the cluster of shopping bags, maybe six or seven of them, filled to the brim with wrapped Christmas presents. That would be an easy place to hide. But after that was the long stretch of hallway to the door of the living room. It would be a challenge to race through there unseen, but the Tree was totally worth it.

He hoped.

Reaching the shopping bags was no problem. Sneaking behind them was a different story. The heavy sacks were pushed up against the wall with not enough room to squeeze through. Jay didn't want to run around in front of them, so he had to climb over the top.

Fortunately the strings and bows and handles made it easy enough to scramble through the piles of gifts. The piles! Either this family was as big as an army, or they were going to have a very, very merry Christmas.

The last shopping bag was Jay's favorite. It was filled with several pairs of brand new Christmas pajamas and socks, all unwrapped but each tied with a bow. At the top of the sack sat a pair of snowpeople slippers, white and puffy and fluffy, one with a cute snowman's face and one with a cute snowlady's face. Their gruff voices, however, were not cute.

"Get off my nose, bub," grunted the snowman slipper.

"Watch out! You almost poked me in the eeeeye!" whined the snowlady slipper.

"So sorry, so sorry!" Jay said, backing up. "I should have known you were talkers. Everything else in this house sure seems to be."

"What're ya doing here? Aren't ya supposed to be in the kitchen?" asked the snowman slipper.

"Yeah, he looks like he belongs in a cookie or a cupcake," said the snowlady slipper.

"No, no, no, no. I'm not that kind of candy

cane. I belong on the Christmas Tree," said Jay.

"The Christmas Tree is for ornaments, bub. You ain't no ornament," said the snowman slipper.

"He's shaped like a hook, though. Ornaments have hooks, ya know," said the snowlady slipper.

"Exactly. I'm perfect for hanging on the Tree. It's where I belong," Jay said with all the confidence he could muster.

"Heh, heh, heh. We belong on a pair of feet, but you don't see us runnin' our mouths off about it," the snowman slipper said.

"You belong in somebody's mouth. Candy canes are for eating, you know," the snowlady slipper said.

"No way, not me!" said Jay. "Now if you'll

pardon me for rushing, I have somewhere else I need to be. Nice meeting the both of you. Merry Christmas!" Then Jay swung onto a ribbon hanging over the edge of the shopping bag.

"Everything has its place, bub," called the snowman slipper. "Remember that."

"Sure thing," Jay said, not looking back.

"And don't forget to wash your feet!" yelled out the snowlady slipper. "No one likes a dirty foot."

"Eew," the snowman slipper said.

Jay dropped to the floor, remembering he was out in the open yet again. He looked around for the cat, but the area was empty. In fact, now there was nothing — absolutely nothing — between him and the doorway into the living room. The Tree was literally right around the corner. But this long stretch of floor looked even longer now that it was right in front of him.

There was nothing else to do; he was going to have to make a run for it.

Chapter Nine

THE
STOCKINGS

He took a deep breath and counted to three. One … two …

And then Princess Poopsie-Fangs pounced. It grabbed him right between its paws. Jay tried wriggling out, but it held him tight. He looked up into its giant, furry face. Its whiskers alone were as long as his whole body. Its yellow eyes stared at him with both contempt and curiosity. Jay stared up at it, waiting for his doom.

But it just looked at him. The cat tilted its head to the side, as if to wonder what Jay was going to do next. After a long moment, he felt its paws loosen a little. He held his breath for an instant, then took half a step backward. Princess Poopsie-Fangs clutched him again. But after a few seconds, it loosened its paws again. This time Jay leaped out and started running. He took nine or ten steps before the cat was on top of him anew, holding him to the ground. But, sure enough, a moment later it lifted its paw. Jay scampered off once more, only to be caught a third time.

Princess Poopsie-Fangs wanted to play.

Okay, thought Jay, trying to catch his breath. I can play this game. As long as we keep it moving toward the Tree.

Though he was relieved not to be dying,

Jay found himself getting tired. The cat was having loads of fun, but Jay was getting worn out, and fast. The door was getting closer, but he wasn't sure how long he could keep this up.

When they finally got within a few steps of the living room, Jay saw his chance. Just inside the door he could see a tall potted plant. If he could leap into the plant, he could hide among the leaves and be out of the cat's reach. It was worth a shot.

Next chance he had, he zigzagged left and right, avoiding the cat's grasp. Two seconds later he was through the door and jumping as hard as he could into the plant. The cat swiped at him again. He sprang onto a higher stem, then again onto another, as Princess Poopsie-Fangs kept pawing for him. Soon he found himself at the top of the plant — it was practically a tree — with nowhere to go but down. The cat sat back on its hind legs and stared at him, swishing its tail back and forth and purring. It wasn't going anywhere.

Jay looked around for somewhere else, anywhere else, to go. Next to the plant was a fireplace with a wide, wooden mantelpiece across the top. Across the front of the mantelpiece hung four Christmas stockings. It was a little far, but Jay thought he could reach the closest stocking if he jumped with all his might.

Jay jumped, barely catching the bottom edge of the stocking. He clung tight as Princess Poopsie-Fangs watched from below. Placing one arm after the other, he climbed up the stocking. When he made it to the top, he slung himself over the edge of the stocking and hung by his hook, finally getting a moment to rest.

It was then that he saw it: the Christmas Tree, in all its splendid glory. It was a big one, round and full and tall and the deepest green Jay had ever seen. It was covered in dozens of glistening glass ornaments and red-and-white bows, spotted here and there with character ornaments like Snoopy, Totoro, and the Cat in the Hat. A galaxy of colored lights shined and blinked, filling the room with a warm, pinkish hue. Golden garland wrapped the Tree in a radiant spiral that led all the way to the top, where a beautiful angel robed in white lace stood, as if queen of all Christmas.

Jay felt a feverish tingle run up and down his body. It was more magnificent than he could ever have imagined. He looked—

"Um, excuse me, but what are you doing?" said a timid voice. It sounded young, like a child.

Jay felt the Christmas stocking squirm. "Oh, please forgive me. I just need to relax for a few minutes, if that's alright with you," he said. "It's been a rough day, and I've been chased by the cat for, gosh, minutes and minutes!"

"Mom," the littlest stocking called out. "There's a candy cane in me."

"Hey, no fair! Why does she get a candy cane and I don't?" said the young stocking next to Jay.

"Calm down, both of you," said the mother stocking. "Santa doesn't fill us up till later tonight."

"What's going on over there?" said the

father stocking. "Don't you know it's nap time?"

Jay peered out to see the other three Christmas stockings straining to get a look at the littlest stocking.

"See! See! There it is! She's got a candy cane! Where's mine? I want a candy cane!" said the boy stocking.

"Where did you get that candy cane, young lady? You don't even know where it's been!" said the mother stocking.

"Did someone say candy cane? Is it Christmas Eve already? Why am I always the last to know these things?" blustered the father stocking.

"I don't mean to be a bother. I was just taking a quick rest while I—"

"It tickles," said the littlest stocking, and let

out a shiver.

"I want a candy cane!" yelled the boy stocking. "I wanna tickle!"

"I don't know who you think you are, but I know for a fact that Santa hasn't come yet. Don't you know anything about Christmas?" the mother stocking scolded him. "That's not where you belong!"

"Look, I can explain. . . ." Jay started to say.

"He smells all pepperminty and stuff," the littlest stocking giggled.

"I wanna smell pepperminty!" the boy stocking shouted.

"Everything has its place, and that is not your place. Santa Claus did not put you there," said the mother stocking.

"Is someone breaking the rules? Just wait till I get my hands on you!" said the father stocking.

"You don't have hands, dear," said the mother stocking.

"This candy cane is my new best friend!" squeaked the littlest stocking.

"I WANT A BEST FRIEND!" cried the boy stocking.

"See what a mess you're making?" said the mother stocking. "For the love of Rudolph, have a little respect for tradition!"

"I can see why they keep you in storage boxes for eleven months out of the year," said Jay. He pulled himself out of the Christmas stocking and leaped up onto the mantelpiece. "Nevertheless, I wish you all a merry Christmas!"

"Come back!" called the littlest stocking.

"I want!" howled the boy stocking.

"Pipe down!" said the father stocking.

"Good riddance," huffed the mother stocking.

Jay waved and trotted toward the other end, hoping he could find a safe way down. He could hear the Christmas stocking family continue to fuss and bicker, but did his best to ignore them. Besides, he was entranced with the Tree.

He couldn't take his eyes off it.

It mesmerized him so much that he wasn't watching where he was going . . . and fell off the mantelpiece to the floor.

Where he snapped in half.

Chapter Ten

THE
GARBAGE

Luckily, Jay's plastic wrapper kept him together. But now he was a broken candy cane. A damaged candy cane. Maybe even a worthless candy cane.

Jay couldn't believe it. He had made it so far. The Tree was so close he could almost touch it. For the longest time he lay there on the floor, speechless, staring at the Tree through the tears in his eyes.

Princess Poopsie-Fangs pranced over to Jay and stared at him, ready for another chase. But he didn't move. It nudged him with its paw, sniffed him, and even gave him a lick or two. Finally the cat gave up and wandered into the hallway for another nap.

Jay wasn't sure if he fell asleep, or if he just let time pass in a mindless blur, but he was jolted out of his stupor when he heard footsteps marching into the room.

"What's this? Who left a broken candy cane on the floor?" yelled the lady. THE lady. The Evil Mistress of Christmas Horrors. "This is not where garbage belongs!" she said, and picked Jay up off the floor. She walked to another room and tossed him in a bin. It was full of bits of ribbon and scraps of wrapping paper. Then she took the bin outside, where she set it next to several other boxes of rubbish.

"What a mess. I'll make the kids sort the recycling after Christmas," she said aloud to herself, then went back inside the house.

Jay lay in the bin, gazing up at the cloudy sky. He shivered from the cold outside. He already missed the warmth and coziness of the house, already missed the endless decorations and chiming carols, already missed a home he never really had.

He was tempted to stay put, to lie there with the trash and be forgotten forever. But if he were going to be forgotten, he could at least have a look around at his final resting place.

Jay sighed and pulled himself up to the rim of the rubbish bin. He saw two large black trash cans overflowing with garbage. Next to them, on the ground, lay boxes and bags and piles of discarded junk. Unwanted things cast away to be unremembered. One box in particular caught his eye: it was full of broken Christmas decorations, including what appeared to be a nativity scene.

He hopped out of his bin to have a closer look. Inside were cracked ornaments, smashed bulbs, a tattered old stocking with a hole in the toe, a ceramic reindeer missing its nose, a miniature Christmas tree bent sideways in the middle, an elf ballerina with only one leg, an angel without a left wing, a tiny stuffed polar bear with fluff sticking out of a split seam in its neck, and a wind-up sleigh that probably didn't wind up anymore, along with a heap of shattered baubles and trinkets across the bottom of the box.

What caught his attention the most, however, was the nativity scene. He could tell it was very old, and must have been at one time a rather majestic scene to behold. But now it was not much more than a dusty collection of broken pieces. Jay took a closer peek at the carnage. The stable was in shambles. Mary was missing her clothes, Joseph was missing his head, and baby Jesus was missing entirely. One of the sheep was half melted, while the other sheep was half legged. The manger — or what was left of it — looked as though it had been chewed by a pack of hyenas. He couldn't tell a difference between the camel and the donkey (or maybe it was a hippopotamus?). Both angels looked more like devils than heavenly creatures. And

the wise men — the only two Jay could see —
had long lost their gifts.

What a mess, Jay thought. For a moment,
he forgot all about his own problems. This
nativity scene was a disaster. It was nothing
more than garbage, and ugly garbage at that.
If anything deserved to be thrown out, it was
this pile of junk.

But it had once been beautiful, he could
tell. Flakes of colorful paint still clung
here and there to bits of the scene and its
characters. The face of one of the angels
looked as divine as it ever had. Even the sheep,
as mangled as they were, were still oddly
charming.

More than that, Jay knew that this nativity
scene had been loved for a long, long time.
It could only be this worn out if it had been

used and re-used and loved and re-loved over and over and over again.

"I wish I could have been loved like that," said Jay aloud.

"That's the wrong wish," said a calm, deep voice from within the rubble.

Chapter Eleven

THE
WISE MAN

One of the two wise men leaned up from where he'd been lying and dusted himself off. He looked at Jay with old eyes that still had a touch of their magical twinkle from years past. His dark skin was scuffed, and his once-resplendent robe was torn and faded. If he'd ever worn a crown or jewels, they were long gone.

"What do you mean, 'that's the wrong wish'? Isn't being loved the best thing in the world?" Jay asked.

"We are all meant to be loved, yes. And it is indeed a great thing. But it is not the greatest thing," said the wise man.

"Then what's the greatest thing?"

"It is not to be loved, but to love. To give love is better than to receive love. Better yet, giving love without expecting any love in return. When you can love like that, everything will be in its right place," the very wise man said.

Everything in its right place. Jay had heard that before, but didn't know what it really meant until just now.

"But I'm broken," Jay said.

"We're all broken. We all need to get better. But you must be broken before you can get better," said the wise man.

Snowflakes began to fall, drifting like specks of powdered sugar on a spiced cake. Jay stood in silence and stared at all the discarded things around him. Now he was one of them. Forgotten and rejected. But did it really have to be this way?

"I'm changing my wish. I don't have much to give, but I'd like to try, at least," said Jay. "I want to love. I'm just not sure how."

"Even a fool can love, my son," said the wise man.

"Do you always speak in platitudes?" Jay asked.

"Heck no. Sometimes I rap! I be spittin' lyrics left and right, blowin' ya mind wit' rhymes all night," the wise man sang. "Yo."

"Okay. . . . But for real, though. What can I do? Where do I start?"

"Can you think of anyone who needs to be loved? Maybe someone who needs it more than anyone else?" asked the wise man.

Jay thought hard as the snow fell harder. A quick look at the dark clouds told him it was going to be a deep, heavy snow, just in time for Christmas day. Soon he and the rest of the rejects would be covered and buried. He glanced again at the wise man, whose tired eyes seemed filled with memories. Yet those memories were likely fading, and would soon be forgotten. The remains of the nativity scene weren't just trash — they were the wise man's friends. His family. His life.

Jay knew at once what he had to do.

"I'll be right back," he said to the wise man.

Chapter Twelve

THE CAT (AGAIN)

When you're busy, time goes by fast. When you're focused, time goes by faster. But when you're showing love to someone, time virtually disappears.

Jay spent the rest of the day staying busy, being focused, and trying to figure out this whole love thing. It was hard work, but he felt good. In fact, he'd never felt better.

But he was running out of time.

Nighttime came quicker than expected, and the snow was piling up. And his crack was getting worse, making it more and more difficult to do what he needed to do. On top of it all, Jay was worried that it was getting too late. The family had gone to bed, and it was time to finish his grand plan . . . or fail.

All his hard work would have been for nothing had he not run into Princess Poopsie-Fangs one more time. Jay was sneaking into the house one last time to find some string. The house was dark and all the lights were out — all except the twinkling lights hanging on the Christmas Tree. He was running toward the kitchen when a giant fluffy tail whacked him in the face. He fell backward onto the floor and nearly cracked again.

"Watch out! You almost broke me in half

again!" Jay muttered. He picked himself up and double-checked to make sure his plastic wrapper was still holding together.

"Sorry about that. I'm usually the only one up this time of night," said the cat.

"Princess Poopsie-Fangs! You can talk?" Jay said. He forgot all about his crack.

"Of course I can talk. I'm not just some dumb piece of chocolate or something."

"Actually. . . ."

"And please stop calling me Princess Poopsie-Whatever. My name is Carl. I'm a dude, you know," said the cat.

"Oh, sorry about that, um, Carl. I'm Jay."

"Thanks for playing with me today, Jay. I haven't had that much exercise in weeks. Made me so tired I slept the whole rest of the day! Phew!" Carl said, yawning.

"Yeah, wore me out, too. Say, I was wondering if you could return the favor for me. I've been working on a secret project all day, and I still need some string. Hopefully a lot of string. Do you know where I could find some?" Jay asked.

"String?! Are you kidding me?! String is my life! It's my catnip, figuratively speaking. 'Cause I'm not into actual catnip. That stuff can kill you. Believe me, I know. I gave it up a long time ago. Been sober for three years. Which is something like 600 dog years. I'm into string now. Much healthier. The organic, fair trade kind, of course. It's really good for you. Did you know that one ball of string can—"

"Carl, I'm kind of in a huge hurry. Maybe you can tell me all about it after Christmas, maybe over a nice bowl of cold milk. But right now I need some string. Can you help me?"

"Jay, today is your lucky day. Follow me," said Carl the cat.

The cat led Jay through the kitchen into the laundry room. In the corner next to the dryer was a carpet-covered cat tree with a pole up the center, a bed at the bottom, a box in the middle, and a platform on the top.

"This is my favorite spot in the whole house. I like sleeping next to the dryer, at least when it's running. So warm. Mmmm. And the low, steady hum just makes me feel all cozy inside. Don't tell the lady, but sometimes I make her clothes dirty just so she'll wash and dry them again. Did you know that dryers—"

"How about that string?" Jay interrupted.

"Right. Be right back." Carl jumped up

into the box and crawled inside. Two seconds later he came out with a ball of twine between his teeth. He dropped the string at Jay's feet.

"That's the good stuff right there," said Carl. "Made from grade-A linen. Imported from Belgium. Only the best."

"Thank you! You're the best cat ever!" said Jay.

"Well, I try not to brag, but yes, yes I am," said Carl, licking his paw.

"I don't suppose I could ask for one more favor? I mean, you're awfully good at them."

"I'm awfully good at a lot of things, if we're just being honest here."

"I've got a box I need to bring in from outside. It's just a few feet from the back door. Should be super easy for a strong cat you," Jay said.

"Whoa, whoa, whoa, little candy dude. First of all, I don't go outside. I'm an indoor cat. Indoor. Cat. Secondly, it's cold and wet out there. If there's one thing cats don't like, it's being cold and wet. And thirdly . . . well, I guess there's just the two things."

"That's too bad. I mean, I thought you looked like the strongest cat I've ever seen. I wasn't sure a cat could even do it. Probably more of a job for a dog. I guess I can see why they called you Princess Poopsie-Fangs," said Jay.

"Now that's low. I see what you're trying to do, sugar stick. Luckily for you, shame works on me. And since it's Christmas, I'm willing to let your mild insult slide. But you'll owe me a favor when this is all over," said Carl.

"Anything. You name it," Jay said. "Now follow me."

Chapter Thirteen

THE
GIFT

The snow had stopped, but several inches covered the ground like a thick layer of white frosting on a birthday cake. A set of paw prints and a wide drag mark made a path from the garbage cans to the back door. Inside the house a trail of wet paw prints ran their way across the shiny wood floor into the living room.

Carl gave himself a thorough shake, sending wet snow in every direction.

"A job for a dog. Hmmph. Well, you were right about that, barber pole. But let it never be said that Carl can't do anything a dog can do," Carl said, then sat on his hind legs and began to lick his fur clean.

"Thank you," Jay said. Then he got busy.

"What're you doing, anyway?" asked Carl. "Not that I care. I'm just curious. Cats are curious, you know. But I am the watchdog around here, since there aren't any actual dogs. Thank GOODNESS. I've got to keep my eye on things, make sure no intruders get in the house. You're not an intruder, are you? Didn't think so. Just between you and me, I'm not sure what I'd do if there was an intruder. Probably hiss at them first. Maybe arch my back a little. Then I'd run off. Not because I'm scared or anything. Pfft. It's not me who's freaked out. It's them who freaks out. They're all like, 'Oh no! Where'd the cat go? I'm gonna die!' I mean, they don't actually say that, but I know they're thinking it."

Jay worked fast while the cat talked. He had never been more tired, but he kept at it.

"So, what exactly are you doing, anyway?" Carl asked.

"I'm putting everything in its right place," Jay said.

"Hmm. I'm no expert or anything, but I'm fairly certain the living room is not the right place for garbage. The lady isn't going to be happy about it. Trash in the house is kind of a big no-no around here. She's very particular. One time she—"

"Carl, can I ask you one last favor?" Jay asked.

"I'm not going outside again," said the cat.

"Do you like peppermint?"

"Never tried it. Is it anything like catnip? 'Cause I'm three-years sober and I really need to stay on the wagon. Not a literal wagon, you know. I'm speaking metaphorically. Just like that whole nine lives thing. Did you know that's actually a metaphor? When they say nine lives, they actually mean—"

"Carl," Jay said, waving his hands. He walked right up to the cat and looked into his whiskery face. "This is very important. I need you to lick me. Make me sticky. I've got to put a few things together," Jay said.

"You know, there's this stuff called glue. It's all kinds of sticky. One time the kids put some glue up their—"

"Carl, please! Glue isn't going to work. It

has to be me. I need you to do this for me, as a friend," Jay said.

Carl stopped cleaning his fur and stared back at the candy cane. "Friend, huh? Well, that's nice of you to say and all. But, gosh. I know what happens to candy when it gets wet. That's not how you want to spend Christmas."

"Christmas isn't about me. It's about love. If I care about Christmas at all, then I have to love," said Jay.

"You're awfully profound for a candy cane," said Carl. "You sure you want to do this?"

Jay nodded. "I'm ready. Do it."

Chapter Fourteen

THE
NATIVITY

You could lick a candy cane once, and no one would probably be able to tell. But if you lick a candy cane again and again and again, it changes. Bit by bit, the stripes disappear. Little by little, it gets smaller and skinnier. And if you lick it enough times, it vanishes completely.

Fortunately, Jay did not vanish. But by the time he had finished using his sticky, sugary self on all the pieces of his special project, there wasn't that much of him left. Jay the candy cane had become Jay the little white stub.

Carl had tried to argue Jay out of it, and even insisted the peppermint was making his eyes water. But Jay wouldn't listen, and stopped only when he was done.

The cat's tongue hung out the side of his mouth. "No offense, but I can't say I enjoyed that. Peppermint isn't my thing. I try to stay away from mint in general. Much too strong, for one thing. And did you know catnip is part of the mint family? Too much of a good thing, if you ask me. I'm more of a savory guy when it comes to flavors. Give me some ginger any day of the week."

Jay was exhausted. He had given everything

he had to give. But he felt good.

For the first time that night, he gazed up at the glorious Christmas Tree. It was truly the most majestic thing he had ever seen. No ornament, decoration, or candy cane could hope for a more magnificent home. But it wasn't going to be his home. Not today, and not ever.

Jay's home now sat beneath the Tree. The nativity scene, fully restored — or, more accurately, remodeled — in its own kind of glory. Though it looked nothing like it did when it had been opened out of its box years and years ago, the nativity scene was a genuine work of art. Jay had talked the broken gingerbread man into becoming a new head for Joseph, as well as donating his broken limbs to the half-legged sheep. He recruited the nutcracker to chop up heaps of chestnuts to give the stable a cozy and enchanting roof. The coal car, covered in bits of shredded yellow candy wrappers, was now the manger, and couldn't be happier. The chocolates were not only excited to be pulled out of their box, they were thrilled to be molded together here and there into hands, feet, little birds, and even a fresh face or two. All the nativity characters had been mended in their own special way, and each one thanked Jay over and over, especially the wise man, who could not be prouder of his sweet little pupil. Perhaps best of all, the broken glass ornaments and other glittering fragments had been glued to the stable and its creatures in a spectacular mosaic. It reflected the Christmas lights in a way that could only be described as magically radiant.

It was a masterpiece.

Jay had used his heart to pull it all together. And then he used himself, literally, to glue it all together.

"It's perfect," said Carl, giving Jay a gentle pat with his paw. "You did good."

"Thanks," said Jay. "Before I take my place, I have a gift for you."

Jay led Carl to a hidden spot behind the Tree. There sat the two snowpeople slippers.

"They're all yours," said Jay. "I hear they make a wonderful cushion. For your butt."

Carl grinned. "Now that is something I can use!" He rubbed his paws together and marched over to the slippers. He began pressing his paws all over their faces and stretching his claws deep into their puffy fluff.

"What's going on?" gasped the snowlady slipper.

"Hey, who do you think you are?" said the snowman slipper.

"You don't belong here!" the snowlady slipper said.

"Getoffme! Getoffme!" the snowman slipper muttered.

Finally the cat plopped his backside down directly on their faces, wiggled his butt back and forth for good measure, and then laid his chin on his front paws.

"Ya gotta be kidding me," mumbled the snowman slipper.

"Goodnight, Jay," Carl said, and fell fast asleep.

Jay smiled and returned to the nativity scene. He grabbed a little square of blue felt and wrapped himself up tight. The he crawled into the coal car, his new permanent bed, and yawned. That night he dreamt, not of Christmas Trees and twinkling lights, but of friends and the sparkles in their eyes.

Chapter Fifteen

THE
RIGHT PLACE

On Christmas morning the children woke first, as usual. When they shook their parents awake to come and see what was under the tree, the mother and father stretched and yawned and thought first of coffee.

"You have to come and look," said the younger child.

"It's our old nativity," said the older child. "Something happened to it."

This was not what the mother expected to hear.

The family staggered into the living room, rubbing their eyes. Then their four jaws dropped wide open.

"Oh my heavens, that's the most adorable thing I've ever seen! Who made this?" asked the mother.

"I dunno," said the older child.

"I break things. I don't make things," said the father, shrugging.

"Musta been Santa Claus," said the younger child.

"Look," said the older child, kneeling on the floor for a closer peek. "It has a new baby Jesus, too. Isn't it cute?"

"Hmm," said the mother. "Someone must really love us."

The wise man smiled.

The coal car beamed.

The chocolates nearly squeaked.

Carl purred.

And Jay was exactly where he belonged.

The End...

Deleted Scenes

The Cookies

"Oh, I almost forgot!" said the mother. "We need to put out the cookies and milk for Santa!"

She and her children got out the special plate and cup they used only once a year. The older child filled the cup with cold milk, while the other got a napkin out of the cupboard. Their mother set out nine candy cane–shaped cookies on the plate. Then they set it all on a little footstool next to the fireplace.

"Will Santa eat all of them?" asked the younger child.

"I hope not," said the mother. "That's a lot of cookies!"

The lights went off and they all went to bed.

It was then that the nine candy cane–shaped cookies began to talk.

"What a trip," said the first candy cane cookie.

"What in the heck just happened?" said the second.

"I think we've been transformed into ... into ... into...." stuttered the third.

"Cookies," said the fourth.

"I think I rather like being a cookie," said the fifth.

"We must still be alive then after all,"

beamed the sixth candy cane cookie.

"No doubt about it," nodded the seventh.

"Gllmmfffpuddlobbrrrr," mumbled the eighth, who still hadn't gotten the talking thing figured out.

"Has anyone seen the pickles?" the ninth one said.

Then, sometime after midnight, there arose a clatter on the roof — prancing and pawing and whatnot. A minute later, two black boots landed in the living room, followed by a jolly old saint with a thick white beard.

"Who's the guy in the red ninja suit," said the first candy cane cookie.

"Heck if I know," the second cookie said.

"He looks an awful lot like ... like ... like...." the third one stuttered.

"Santa Claus," the fourth said.

"Do you think he's robbing the place?" wondered the fifth.

"More like adding unnecessary junk to the place," the sixth cookie said.

"No doubt about it," the seventh one agreed.

"Sshhhrrrmmmafffurrrbblabburrbblah," added the eighth, nodding.

"Hey you! Got any pickles?" shouted the ninth.

Just then, the jolly old saint spotted the cookies and milk sitting on the footstool. He picked up the plate of cookies and grinned through his beard.

"Peppermint cookies! Ho, ho, ho! My favorite!"

And he ate them all up.

The Chestnuts

Slowly but surely, Jay's plan was coming together. So far he'd managed to avoid being seen by the lady and that darn cat, but he was also running out of daylight. He didn't know how soon his luck might run out.

He'd figured out everything except the stable itself. It was scratched and dented and banged up far more than your average stable. A fresh coat of paint wasn't going to be nearly enough, and, besides, a paint brush was too big for him to hold. Also, he didn't have any paint.

But he did find a bowl full of chestnuts. And he had an idea.

Jay ran back to the nutcracker, who remained faithfully at his post by the potted plant.

"Excuse me, Mr. Nutcracker, I was wondering if you could do me a favor?" Jay asked as politely as he could.

"A favor? For you, the deserter? I most certainly will do no such thing," said the nutcracker as pompously as he could.

"Look, I'm trying to do something nice for a change. It's not even for me. Mostly. But it's a really super nice thing for some old Christmas decorations, such as yourself," Jay said.

"I am not a Christmas decoration. And I am not old," said the nutcracker.

"Right. You're absolutely right. You are definitely not a decoration. You, kind sir, are a bona fide nutcracker. The finest I've ever seen. And the biggest, too! I mean, wow. You are just one giant nutcracker of awesomeness!"

"Your flattery will not work on me. I am a professional."

"But it's for a good cause. There's this old nativity scene that's being thrown away with the garbage. But it really is—"

"No. That is my final answer," said the nutcracker. He sniffed, raised his chin, and stared straight ahead into empty space.

"Oh. Dang. Well, sorry to bother you. Have a merry Christmas anyway," Jay said, hanging his head. As he began to walk away, he muttered, rather forlornly, "I guess I'll just have to find someone else to crack that giant bowl of chestnuts."

The nutcracker snapped his jaw.

Jay spun around. "Sorry, did you say something?"

The nutcracker furrowed his big bushy eyebrow. "I beg your pardon. Merely a . . . sneeze. Although I thought I may have heard someone say something about, er, chestnuts."

"Oh, please don't worry about that. I got a big bowl full of chestnuts back in the living room, and I need to crack them all open and crush them to bits. But I can see you're super busy right now. Anyway, I think I saw a miniature nutcracker ornament hanging on the tree. A Darth Vader one. Pretty cool. I bet he could do it."

"That Sith Lord is no nutcracker, dear sir. He couldn't even fit a single chestnut in his tiny little mouth. A sunflower seed, perhaps. But—"

"Well, I gotta figure something out, since you're so busy and all. I'm sure staring out into empty space is very important," said Jay, who began to walk away again.

The nutcracker cleared his throat. "Dear sir, I apologize for my poor manners. Please forgive my incivility. I would be utterly honored to help you with your chestnuts."

Jay smiled. "Great! Let's get cracking!"

The Snow Globe

"Psst!"

Jay stood atop the mantelpiece, trying to ignore the cries of the Christmas stockings. As he tiptoed his way to the other side, looking for a safe place to get down, he heard it again.

"Pssssst!"

Jay tried to ignore it, but the sound only got louder.

"Pssssssssssstttttt!"

Right behind him was a large snow globe. Inside was a little Christmas beach scene, with a palm tree decked out in a string of lights and surrounded by presents. Next to the beach was a surfer riding atop a wave. Tiny flakes of fake snow floated all around.

"Are you talking to me?" Jay asked.

"Dude! You gotta get me outta here! I'm freezing my tushie off!" said the tiny surfer man inside the snow globe.

"Get you out of there?"

"All they gave me was a swimsuit and a Santa hat. It's SNOWING in here, for Frosty's sake! I'm COLD, man!"

"Is there a door or something?" Jay asked.

"There's no doors in snow globes, genius," said the tiny surfer.

"If you're cold, I could find you a blanket

or something."

"Just push me. Push me off this ledge and then I'll fall and break open and then I'll be free!"

"Fall and break!? That sounds terrible! I'm not doing that," said Jay.

"C'mon, dude! Surfer dudes don't belong in the snow! Just push me FOR THE LOVE OF ALL THAT IS GOOD AND SANDY!"

"I just don't think that's a good idea. I mean, if I fell off of here, that would be the end of it. My life would be over. There's nothing worse than a broken candy cane."

"Don't you think you're being a bit dramatic, bro?" said the tiny surfer.

"Besides, I'm pretty sure that's not actual snow in there. It's probably just tiny pieces of … of … shredded coconut. Yeah, that's it.

You're not even in a snow globe. It's more like a tropical coconut globe!" Jay said with a fake smile.

"Huh," said the tiny surfer. He looked around the snow globe for a moment, thinking. Then he adjusted his swim trunks, threw off his Santa hat, and shouted, "OMG it's hot in here! I'm practically boiling to death! You've got to get me out!"

Also by Jeff White:

Rayjak and the Devil's Halo
Rayjak and the Ring of Hammers
The Astonishing Secrets of Saint Hickory

Made in the USA
Middletown, DE
30 November 2020